W9-BRX-900

An Original Tale by Marguerite W. Davol

How Snake Got His Hiss

illustrated by Mercedes McDonald

Orchard Books / New York

For Jane, who *isss* invincible — M.W.D.

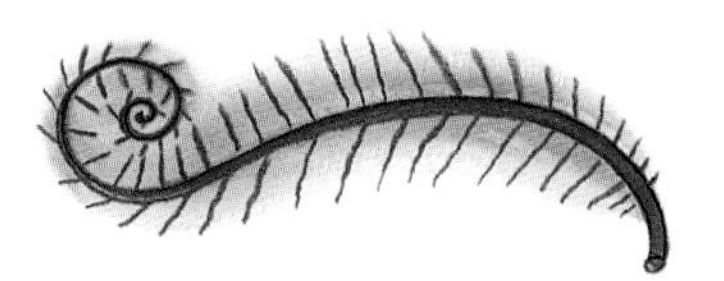

For Kimpy, Toughie, Chichi,
and all the other snake lovers — M.M.

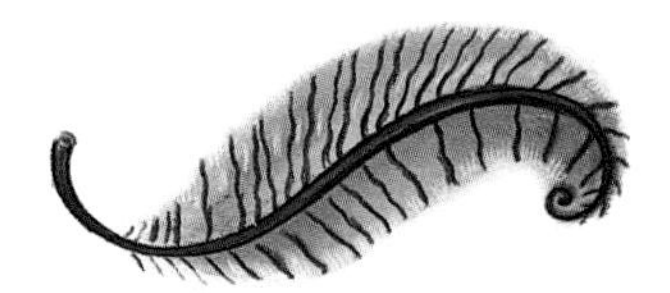

Orchard Books
95 Madison Avenue
New York, NY 10016

Manufactured in the United States of America
Printed by Barton Press, Inc. Bound by Horowitz/Rae
Book design by Chris Hammill Paul

10 9 8 7 6 5 4 3 2 1

The text of this book is set in 13 point Sierra. The illustrations are pastel.

Library of Congress Cataloging-in-Publication Data
Davol, Marguerite W.
How snake got his hiss : an original tale / by Marguerite W. Davol : illustrated by Mercedes McDonald.
p. cm.
"A Melanie Kroupa book"—Half t.p.
Summary: Explains how long ago a self-absorbed snake became responsible for the hyena's spots, the lion's mane, the monkey's chattering, and the ostrich's speed, and its own unique shape.
ISBN 0-531-09468-5. — ISBN 0-531-08768-9 (lib. bdg.)
[1. Snakes—Fiction. 2. Animals—Fiction. 3. Africa—Fiction.] I. McDonald, Mercedes, ill. II. Title.
PZ7.D32155Ho 1996
[E]—dc20 94-45917

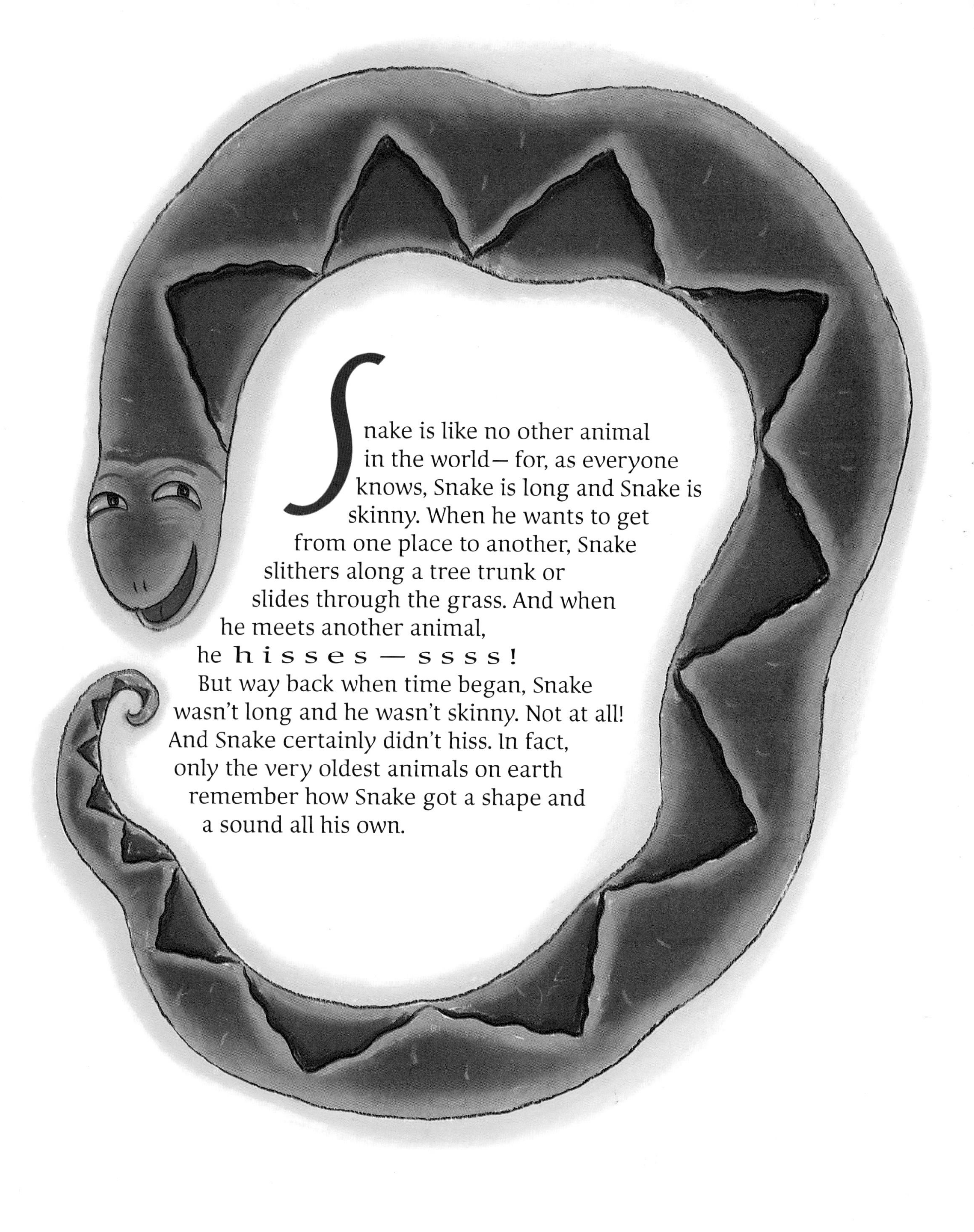

Snake is like no other animal in the world— for, as everyone knows, Snake is long and Snake is skinny. When he wants to get from one place to another, Snake slithers along a tree trunk or slides through the grass. And when he meets another animal, he **h i s s e s — s s s s !**

But way back when time began, Snake wasn't long and he wasn't skinny. Not at all! And Snake certainly didn't hiss. In fact, only the very oldest animals on earth remember how Snake got a shape and a sound all his own.

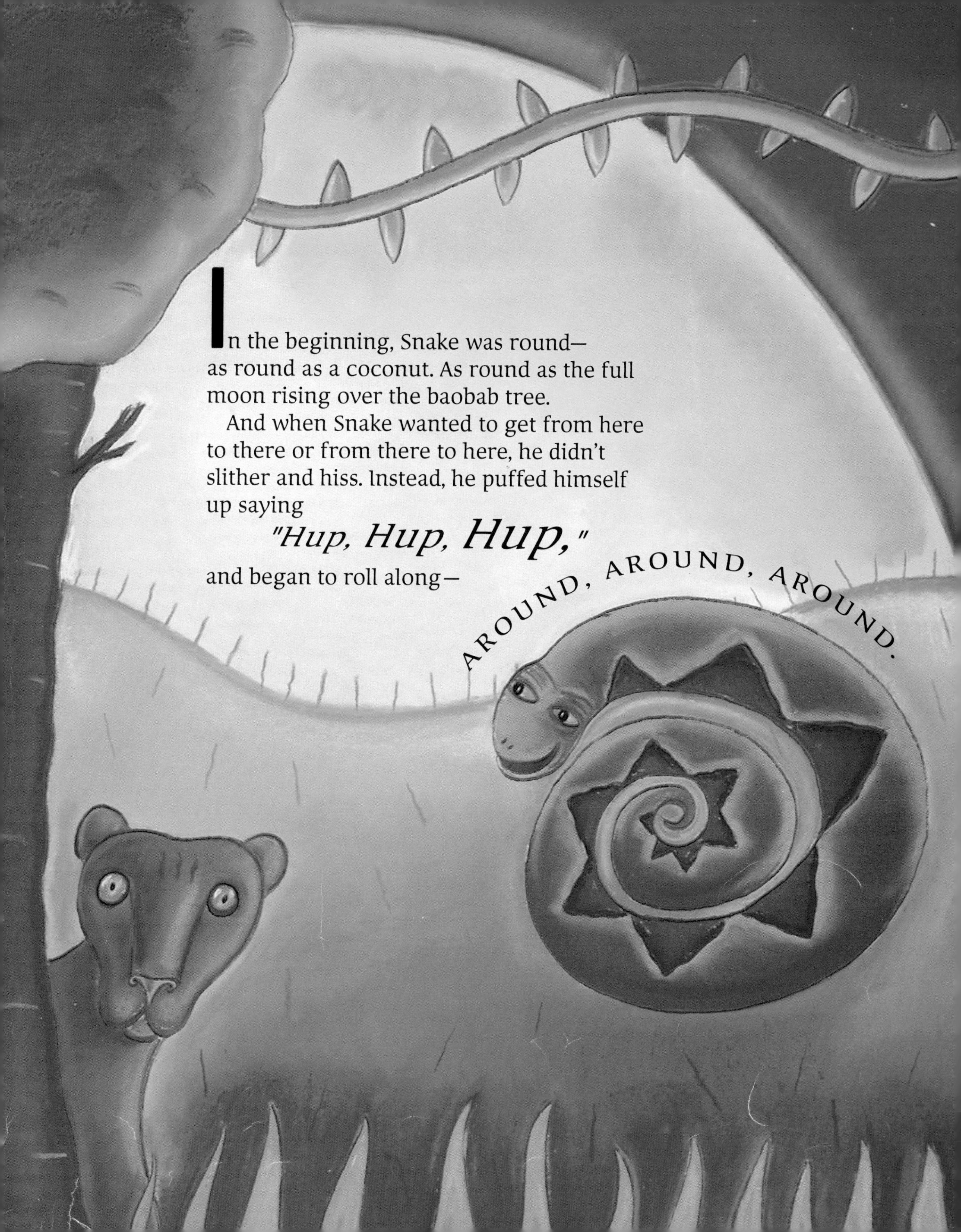

In the beginning, Snake was round—
as round as a coconut. As round as the full
moon rising over the baobab tree.

And when Snake wanted to get from here
to there or from there to here, he didn't
slither and hiss. Instead, he puffed himself
up saying

"Hup, Hup, Hup,"

and began to roll along—

AROUND, AROUND, AROUND.

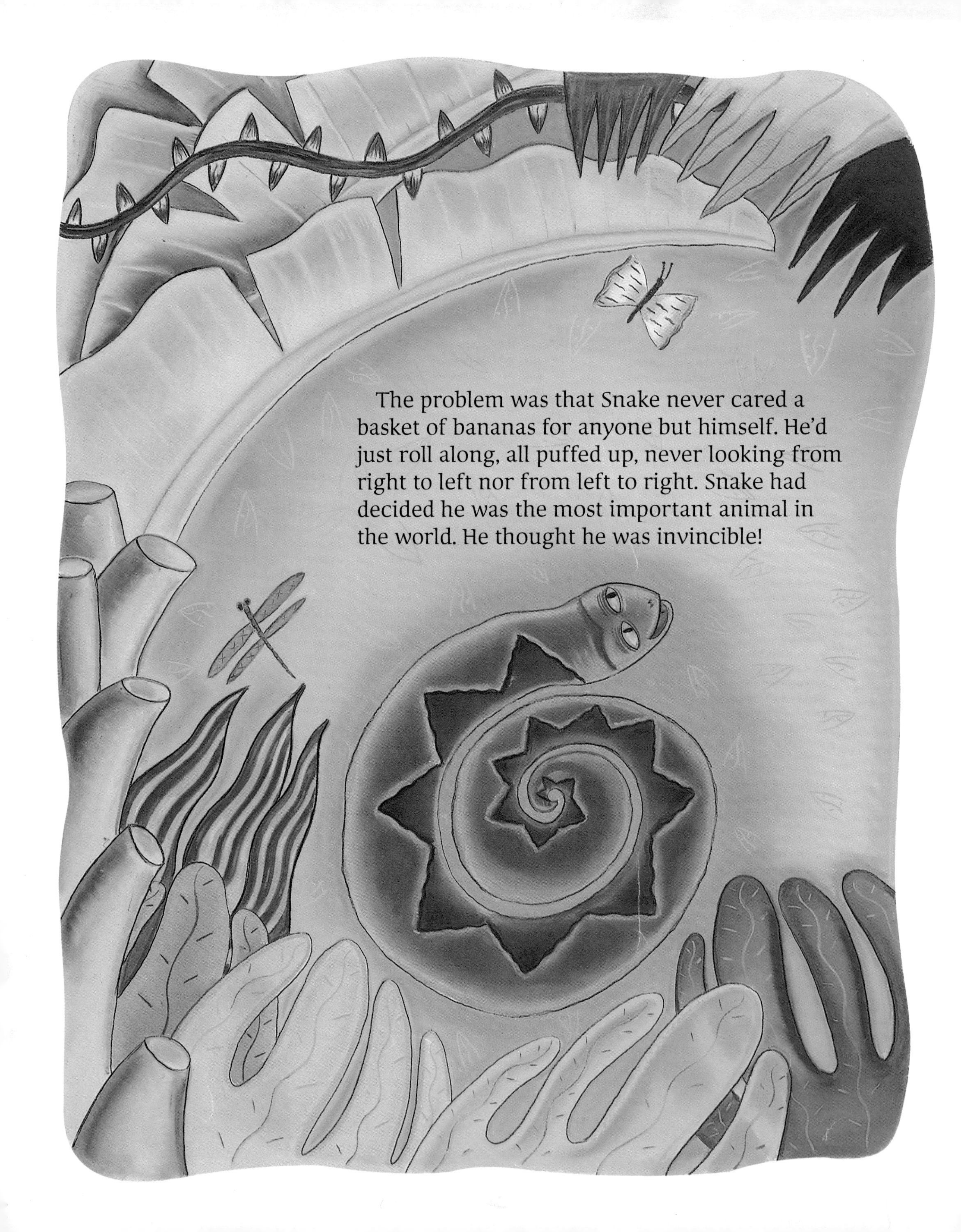

The problem was that Snake never cared a basket of bananas for anyone but himself. He'd just roll along, all puffed up, never looking from right to left nor from left to right. Snake had decided he was the most important animal in the world. He thought he was invincible!

One day, after a heavy rain, Snake was rolling along the forest path—

AROUND, AROUND, AROUND

—all puffed up with his own importance.

From a different direction, hungry Hyena was skulking along the path, looking for prey.

At the very same second, Hyena and Snake came to opposite sides of an enormous mud puddle.

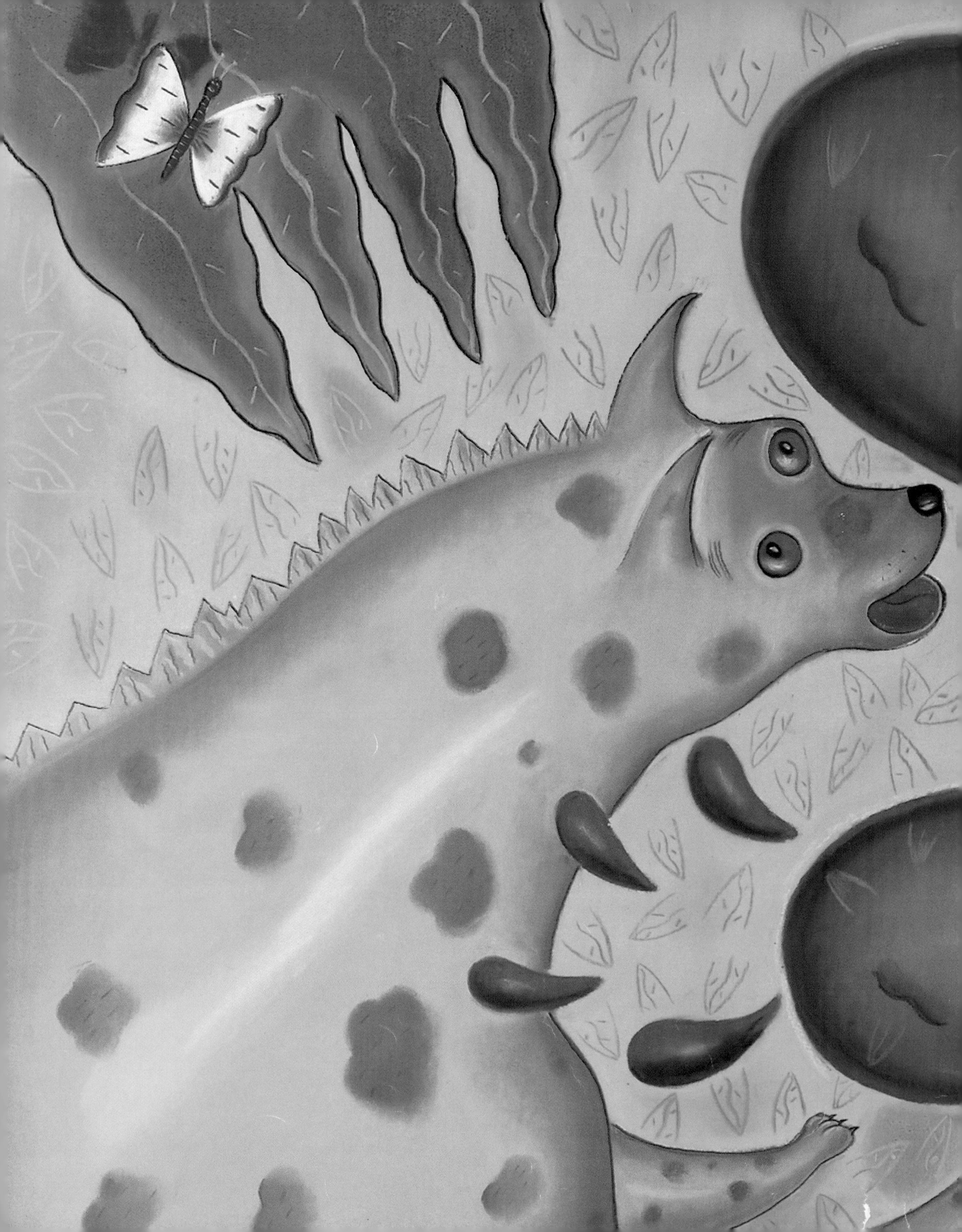

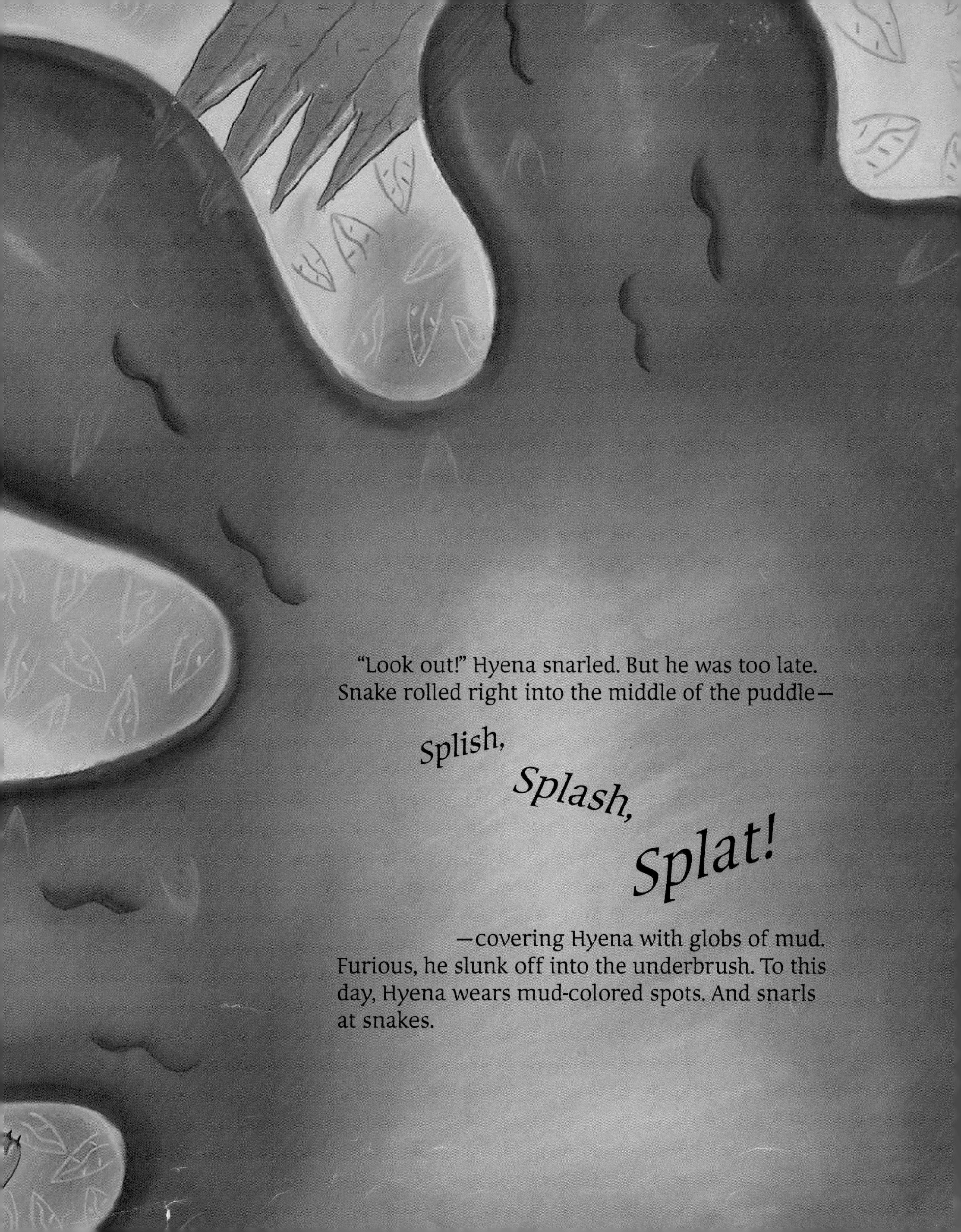

"Look out!" Hyena snarled. But he was too late. Snake rolled right into the middle of the puddle—

Splish,

Splash,

Splat!

—covering Hyena with globs of mud. Furious, he slunk off into the underbrush. To this day, Hyena wears mud-colored spots. And snarls at snakes.

Did Snake watch
where he was going
after that? Not at all.
Rolling along
the path—
AROUND, AROUND, AROUND

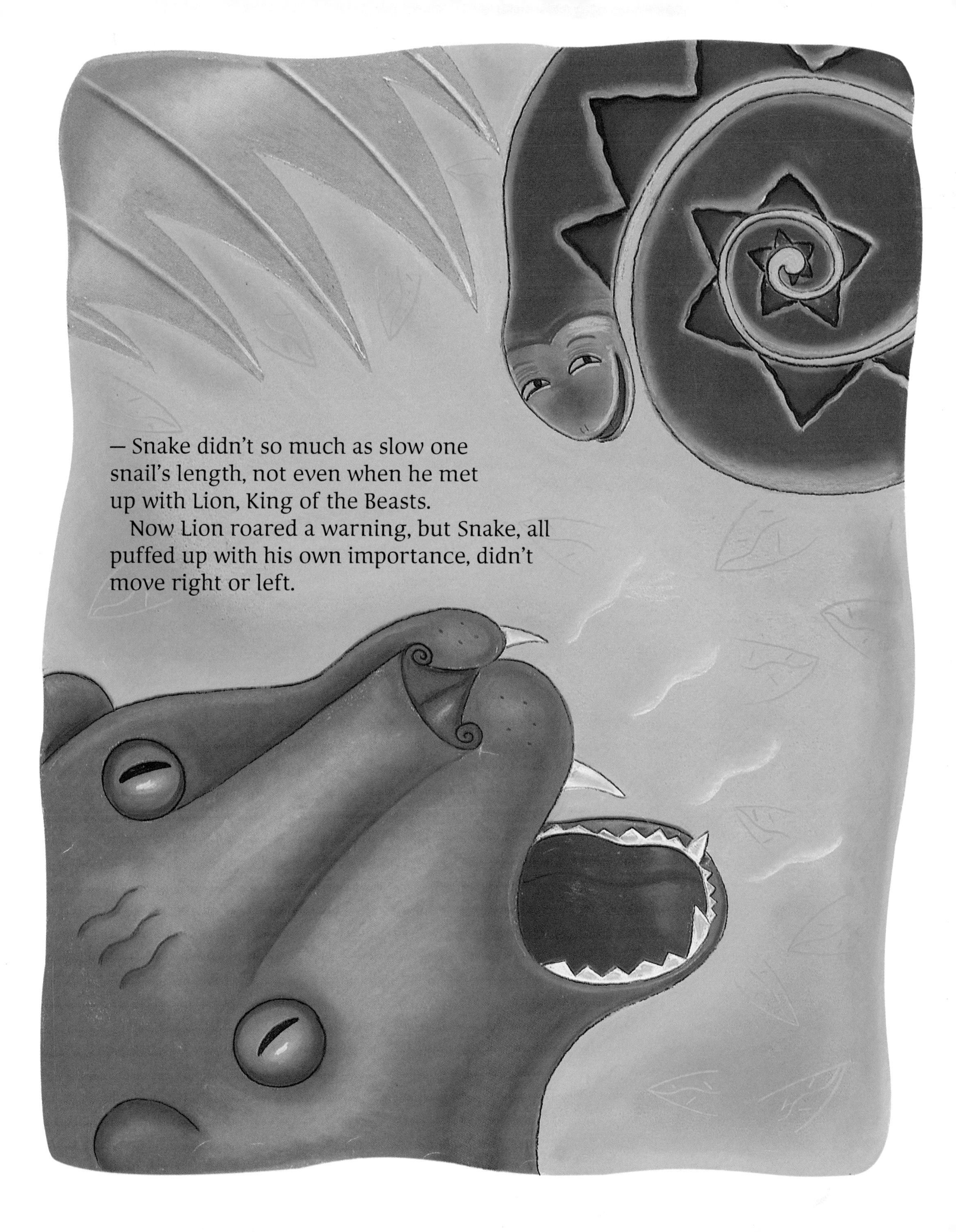

— Snake didn't so much as slow one snail's length, not even when he met up with Lion, King of the Beasts.

Now Lion roared a warning, but Snake, all puffed up with his own importance, didn't move right or left.

Instead, Snake whooshed right between Lion's legs and smack into a termite mound —

Lion was so startled by Snake that the hair all around his face stood on end—sprouting a magnificent mane that Lion still wears today.

As for Snake, he hit that termite mound with such a WHOMP, he was flattened on one side. From then on, whenever Snake wanted to go from north to south or from south to north, he puffed himself up saying

"Hup, Hup, Hup,"

but now, instead of

AROUND, AROUND, AROUND,

he thumped along—

kathumb,

kathumb,

kathumb.

Did that teach Snake to look out for others? Not at all.

A few days later, Snake was thumping along the forest path when he came to a large savanna where the grass stretched from the edge of the rain forest to the end of the sky. As usual, he didn't look up or down but kept moving out into the grass—

kathumb, kathumb, kathumb

—right toward Ostrich, who was standing there stretching to snatch a bingle berry.

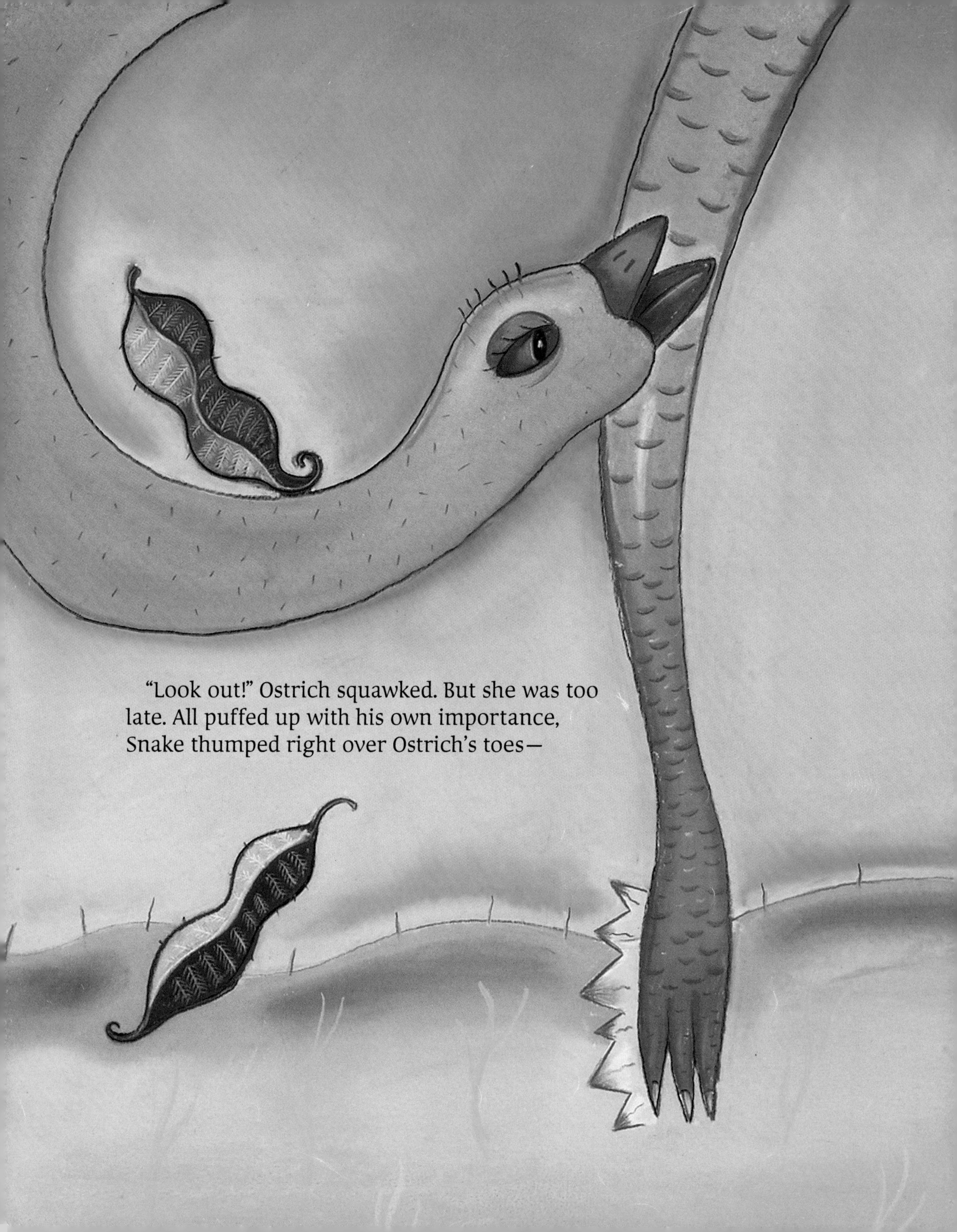

“Look out!” Ostrich squawked. But she was too late. All puffed up with his own importance, Snake thumped right over Ostrich’s toes—

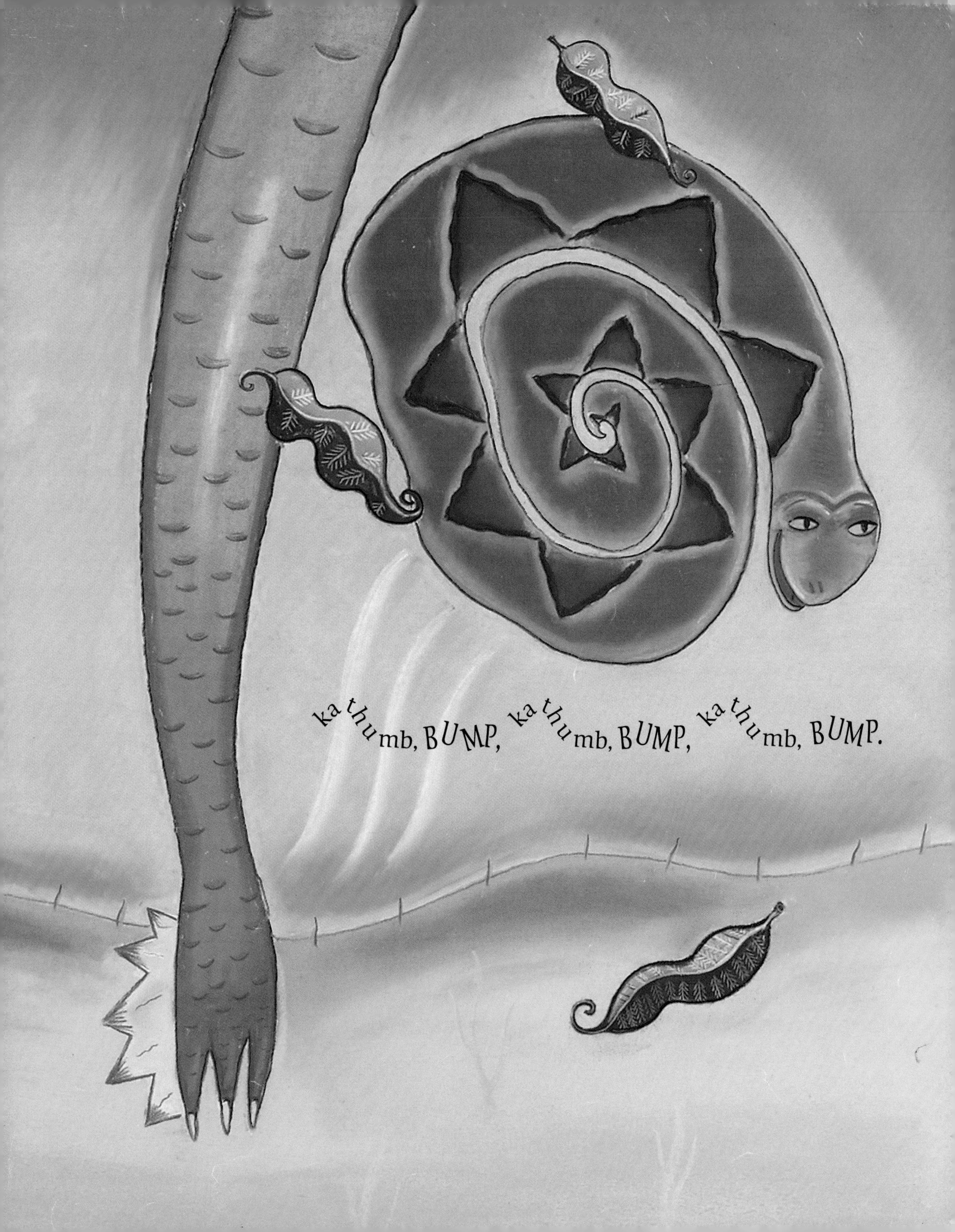
ka thumb, BUMP, ka thumb, BUMP, ka thumb, BUMP.

"YEOW-WOW!" Ostrich howled. Did her feet hurt! They hurt so much that she tried to fly straight up into the air. However, Ostrich's wings were tiny, too tiny to lift such a big bird. So she started to run instead, faster and faster across the savanna. To this day, Ostrich is one of the fastest runners on earth.

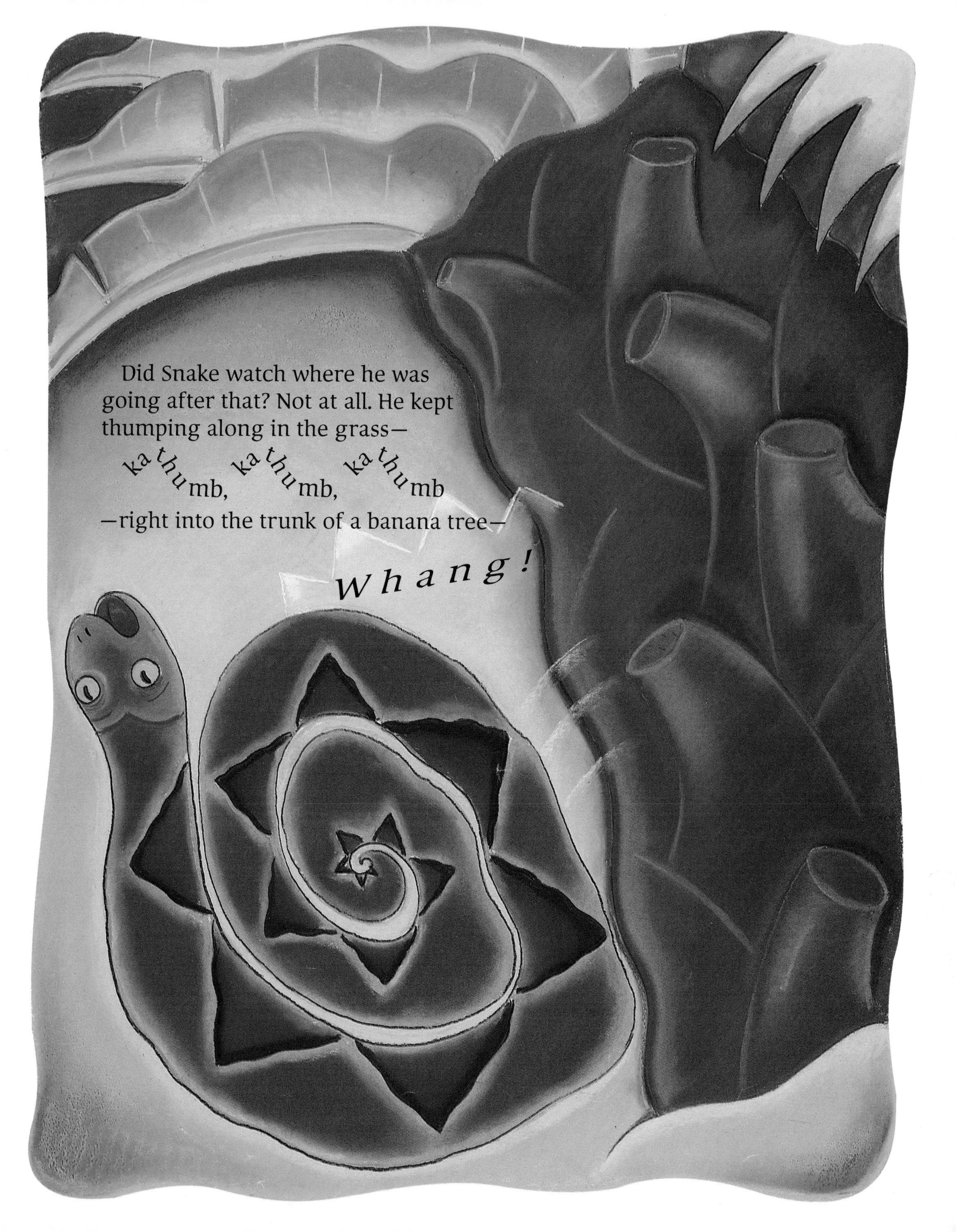

Did Snake watch where he was going after that? Not at all. He kept thumping along in the grass—

kathumb, kathumb, kathumb

—right into the trunk of a banana tree—

Whang!

In the treetop, Monkey had just picked a bunch of bananas. When Snake hit the tree, Monkey was so startled he dropped those bananas—

Plop!

— right onto Snake. Upset about losing his lunch, Monkey began to chatter and leap from tree to tree, just as he does today.

As for Snake, that bunch of bananas made little bumps all over him. And from then on, whenever Snake wanted to go from east to west or from west to east, he puffed himself up saying

"Hup, Hup, Hup,"

but instead of

AROUND, AROUND, AROUND

or kathumb, kathumb, kathumb,

he bumped along—

pockety, pockety, pockety.

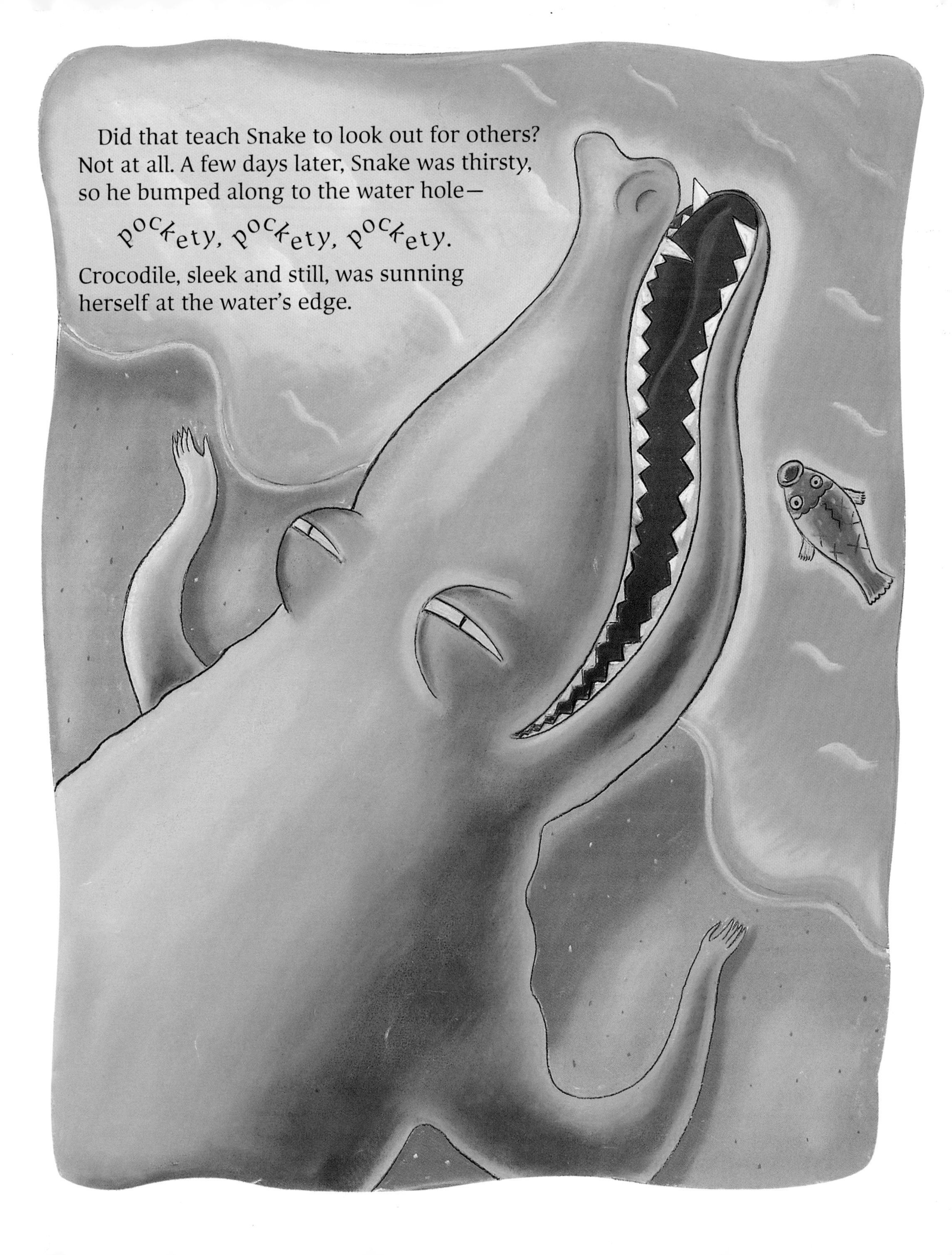

Did that teach Snake to look out for others? Not at all. A few days later, Snake was thirsty, so he bumped along to the water hole—

pockety, pockety, pockety.

Crocodile, sleek and still, was sunning herself at the water's edge.

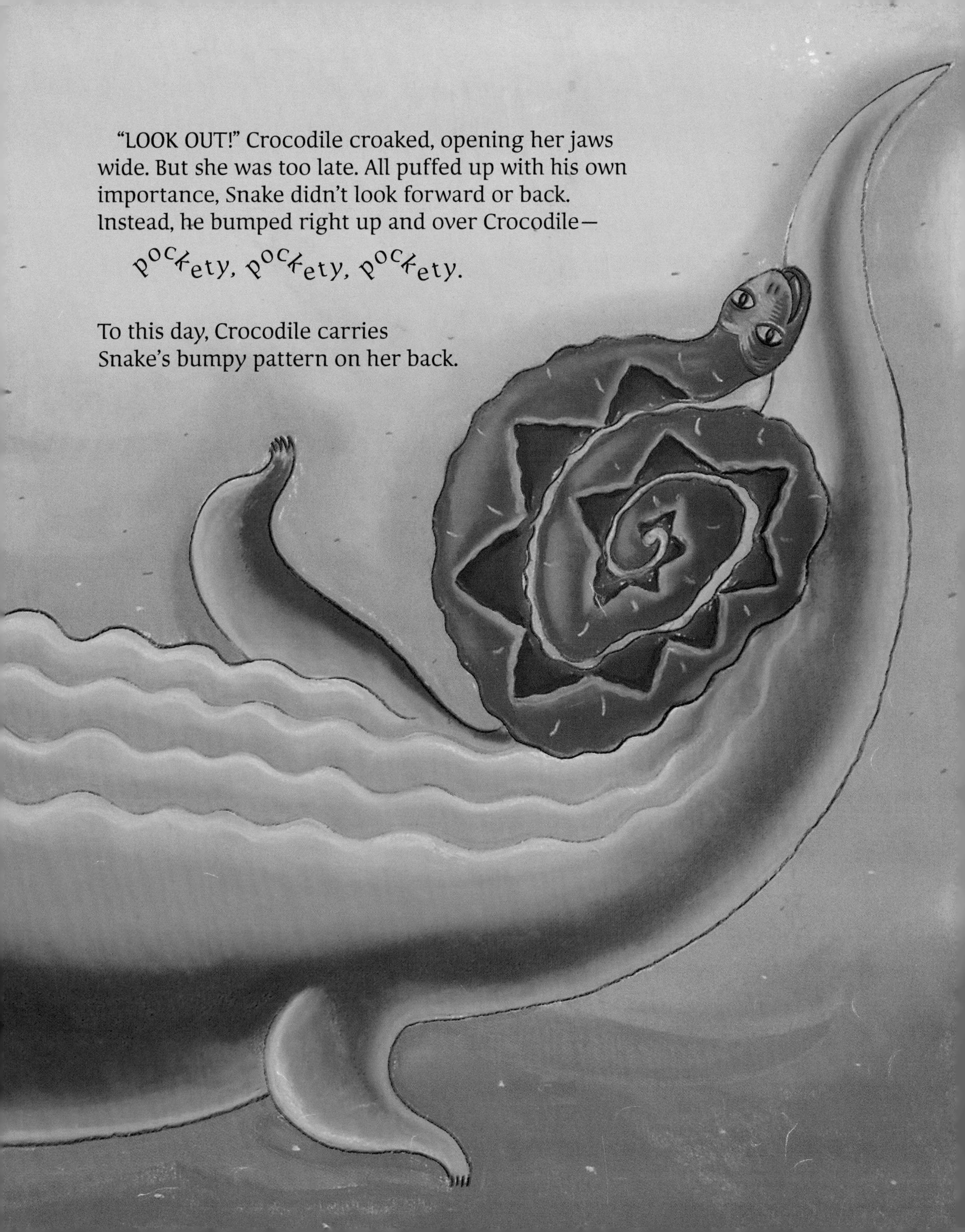

"LOOK OUT!" Crocodile croaked, opening her jaws wide. But she was too late. All puffed up with his own importance, Snake didn't look forward or back. Instead, he bumped right up and over Crocodile—

pockety, pockety, pockety.

To this day, Crocodile carries
Snake's bumpy pattern on her back.

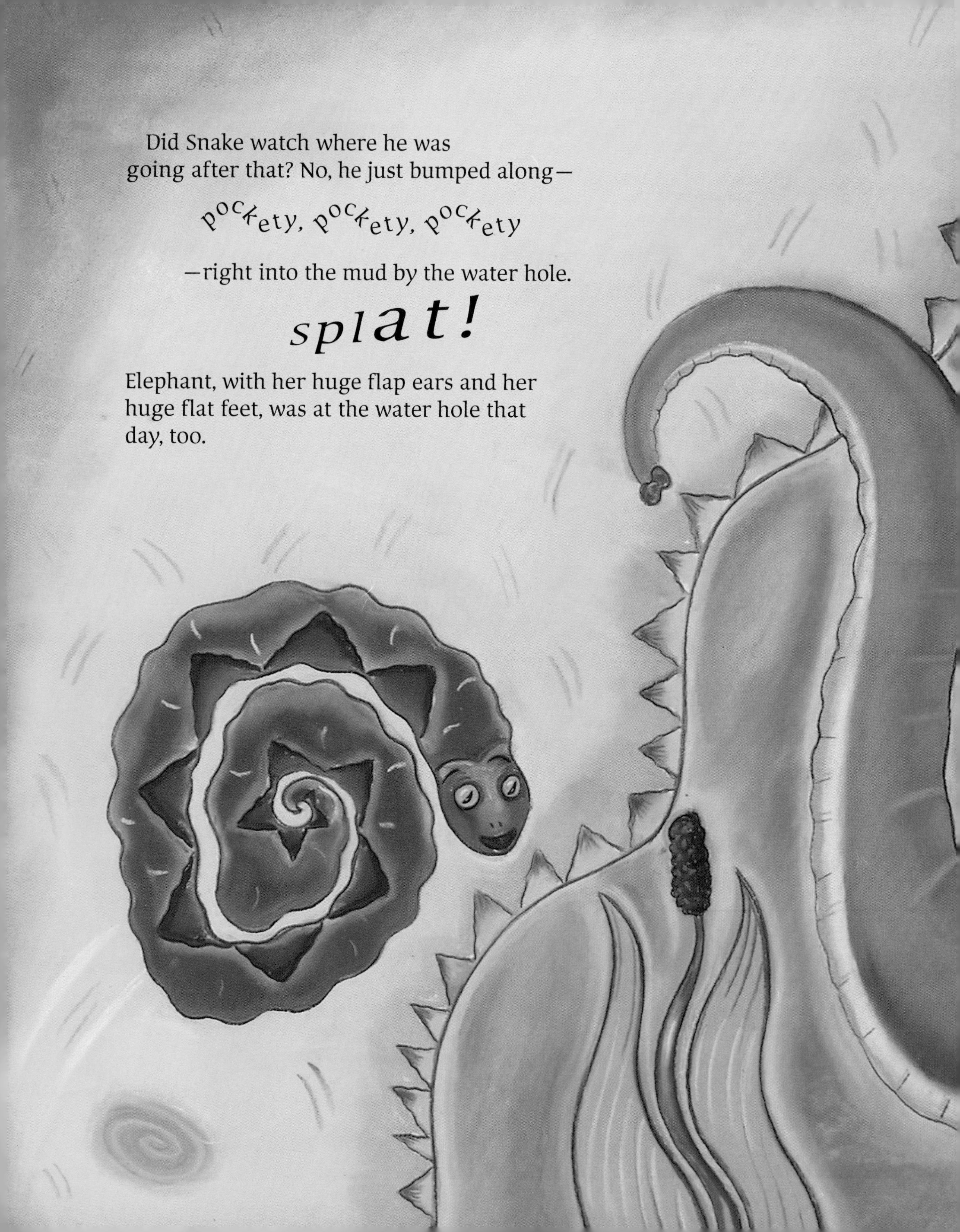

Did Snake watch where he was going after that? No, he just bumped along—

pockety, pockety, pockety

—right into the mud by the water hole.

splat!

Elephant, with her huge flap ears and her huge flat feet, was at the water hole that day, too.

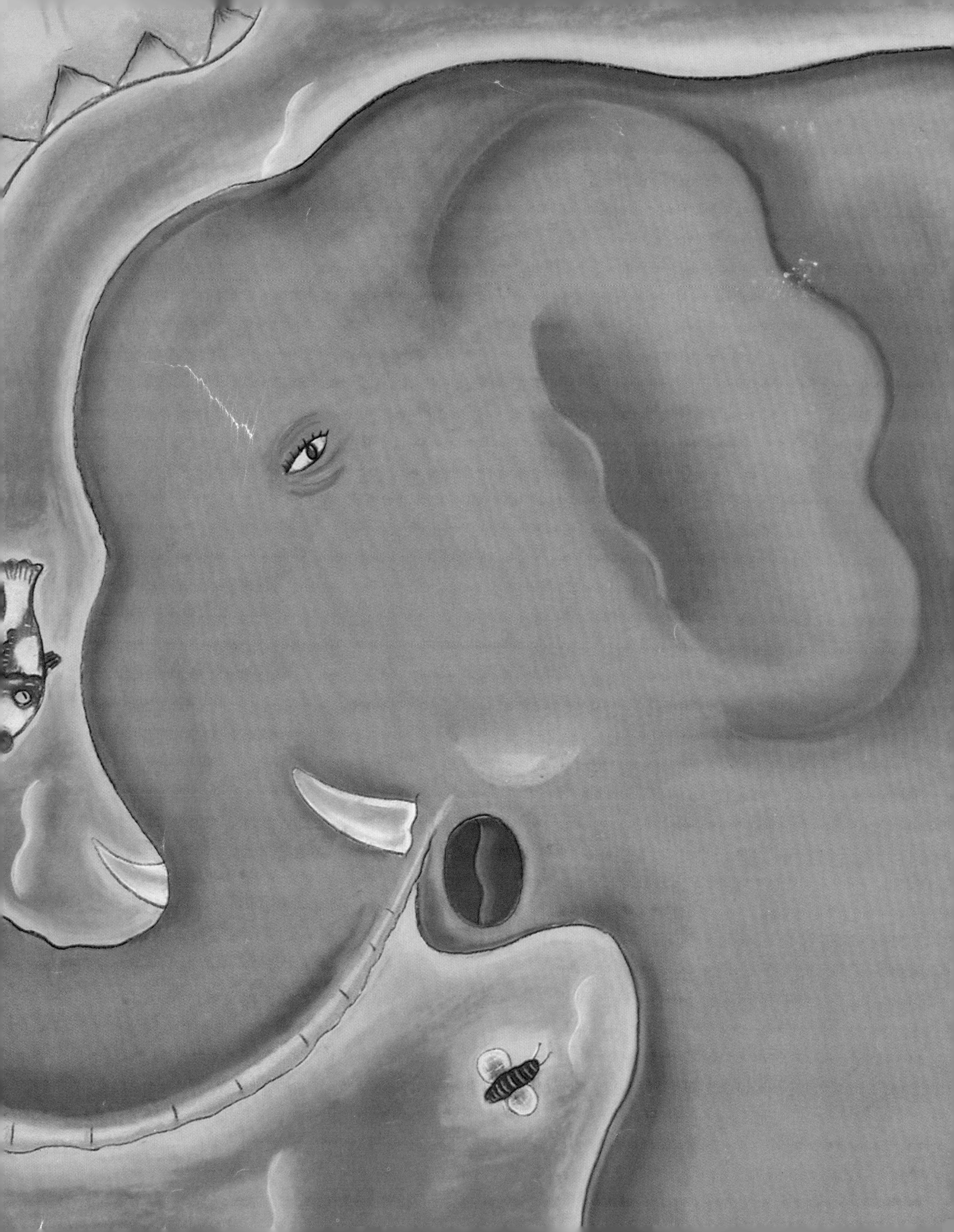

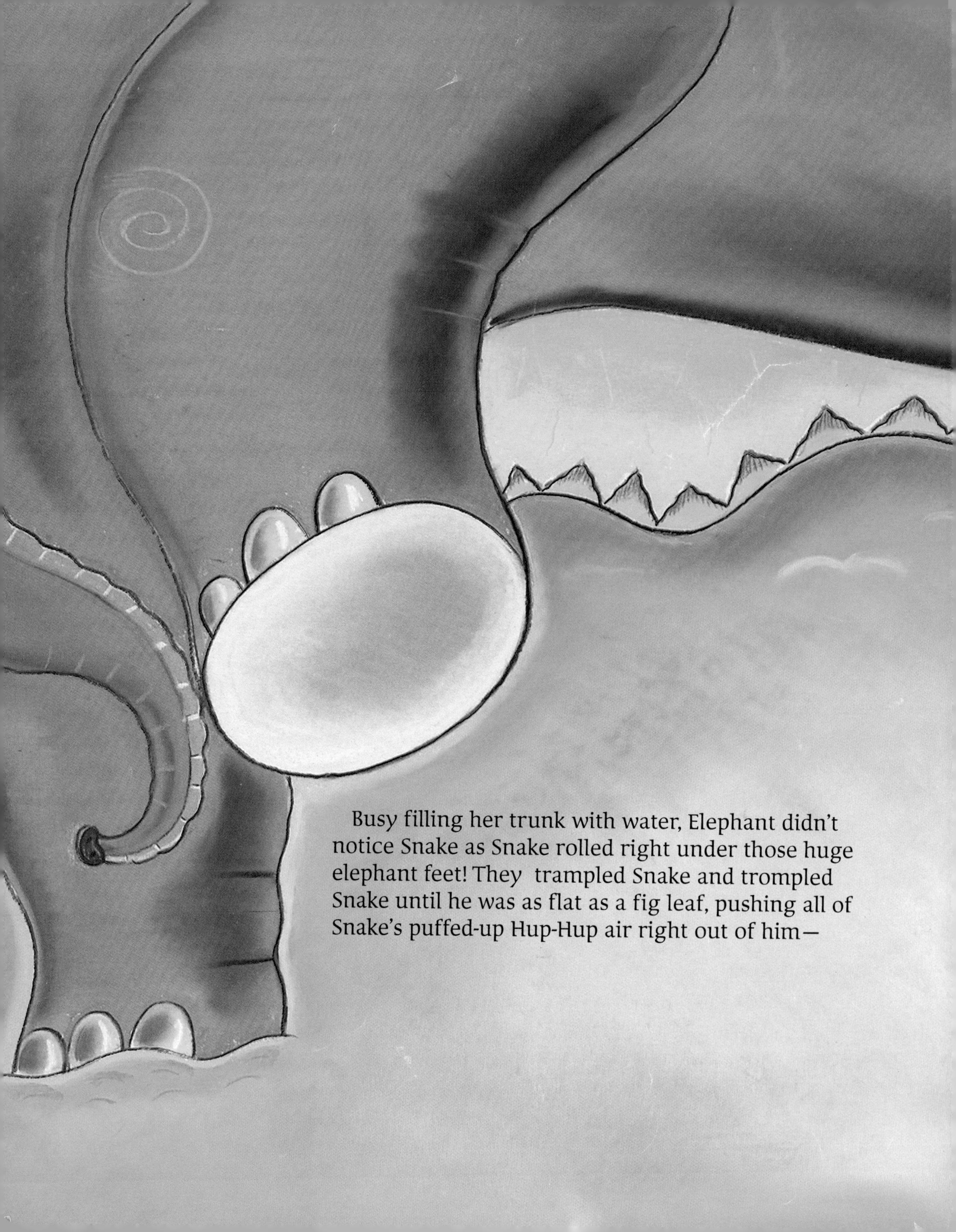

Busy filling her trunk with water, Elephant didn't notice Snake as Snake rolled right under those huge elephant feet! They trampled Snake and trompled Snake until he was as flat as a fig leaf, pushing all of Snake's puffed-up Hup-Hup air right out of him—

Hiss, SSSS, HISS.

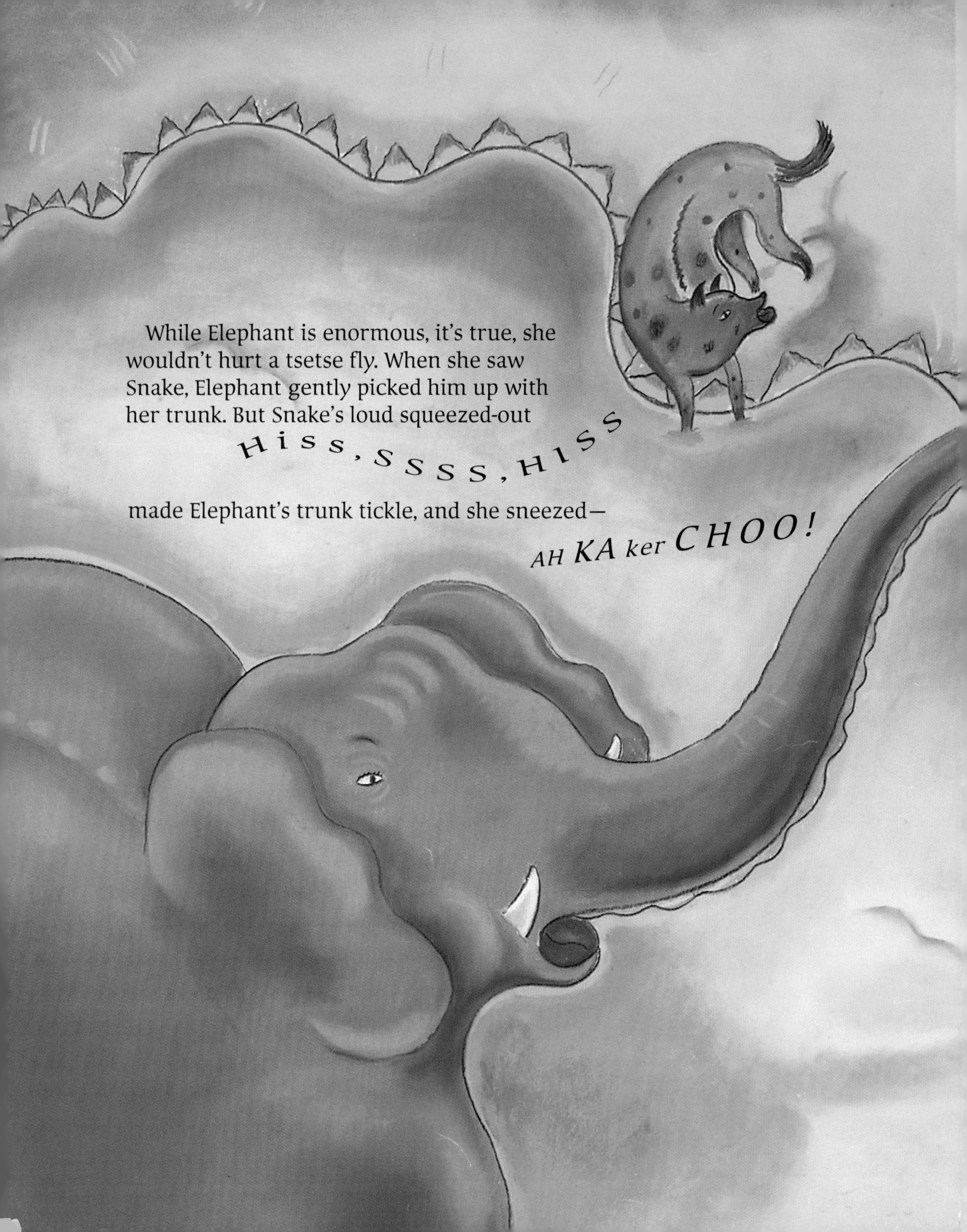

While Elephant is enormous, it's true, she wouldn't hurt a tsetse fly. When she saw Snake, Elephant gently picked him up with her trunk. But Snake's loud squeezed-out

HISS, SSSS, HISS

made Elephant's trunk tickle, and she sneezed—

AH KA ker CHOO!

Snake spiraled
through the air,
Hiss-SSS-ing
all the while. Head
chased by tail, Snake
stretched out, out, out, Out...

until he
became
longer and
thinner than
Elephant's trunk.
To this day, Snake's
shape is long
and thin.

Now, whenever Snake wants to get
from near to far or from far to near,
he doesn't go

AROUND, AROUND, AROUND

or kathumb, kathumb, kathumb

or pockety, pockety, pockety.

He wriggles along instead. And
whenever Snake tries to puff himself up
saying

"Hup, Hup, Hup,"

he's so skinny he can only

HISS, SSSS, HISS.

Has Snake learned to look out for others?
Well, perhaps he has. When he meets
another animal today, Snake hisses and
slithers the other way —

FASSST!